This story is dedicated to every otter who dares to jump out of the water.
May your days be filled with extraordinary adventures.

— K.J.W.

Dedicated to dearest Sammy, our Shetland sheepdog —
a faithful and wonderful companion to us both.

— J.B.B.

Sleeping Bear Press™

315 E. Eisenhower Pkwy., Suite 200
Ann Arbor, MI 48108
www.sleepingbearpress.com

Printed and bound in the United States.

10 9 8 7 6 5 4 3 2 1

Library of Congress Cataloging-in-Publication Data

Wargin, Kathy-jo.
Otter out of water / by Kathy-jo Wargin ; illustrated by John
Bendall-Brunello.
pages cm
Summary: "A playful otter follows two children home and eats popcorn
for lunch, swings on the curtains, and eventually encounters the ranger
who reminds everyone this otter belongs in the water"— Provided by publisher.
ISBN 978-1-58536-431-2
[1. Stories in rhyme. 2. Otters—Fiction. 3. Humorous stories.]
I. Bendall-Brunello, John, illustrator. II. Title.
PZ8.3.W2172Ott 2014
[E]—dc23
2013024889

Otter
Out of
Water

Kathy-jo Wargin

Illustrated by

John Bendall-Brunello

Sleeping Bear Press™
PUBLISHER

Have you seen an **otter**
at play in the **water**?
It's long and it's **trim**
and it knows
how to **swim**.
It rolls and it **spins**.
It twists and it **grins**.

But what if that otter
jumps OUT of the water?
Would you shout hip-hooray?
Would you ask him to play?

Would you clap?
Would you **stomp**?
Would you go for a **romp**?
What if that **otter**
jumps out
of the **water**?

Now what if that otter
stays out of the water?
Would you scamper uphill,
then slide down in a spill?

Would you ride on your bellies
with great otter **skill**?
Would you both get **muddy**?
Would he call you **Buddy**?
What if that otter stays
out of the water?

Now what if that otter follows you home?
Will you hop, will you **skip**?
Will you whistle and **yip**?

Would you hide in the bushes
to give him the **slip**?
What if that otter follows you home?

And what if that otter is right on your heels?
Will you run, will you jog,
will you jump like a frog?
Will he follow you through an old hollow log?
What if that otter is right on your heels?

Now what if the otter
sneaks through the door?
Would you toss him OUT?

Would you tap his **snout**?

Would you give him a bucket of minnows and **trout**? What if that otter sneaks right through the door?

What if the otter
remains in your house?
Would he bounce
on the **chairs**?
Would he skid
down the **stairs**?

Would he swing on the curtains that hang in neat **pairs**?

Do you think an otter belongs in the house?

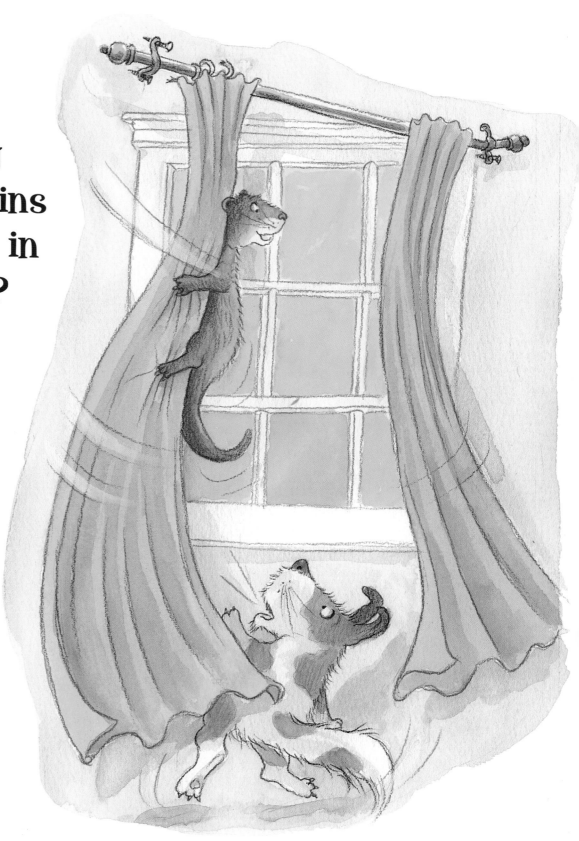

What if that otter wants popcorn for **lunch**?
Would you let him **munch**?
Would he like the **crunch**?

If that otter gets thirsty
will you get him
some **punch**?

What if that otter wants popcorn for **lunch?**

And what would you do when it's time to wash up?
Will you give him a scrub
in your mom's kitchen **sink**?
Will he wear a cap that is puffy and **pink**?

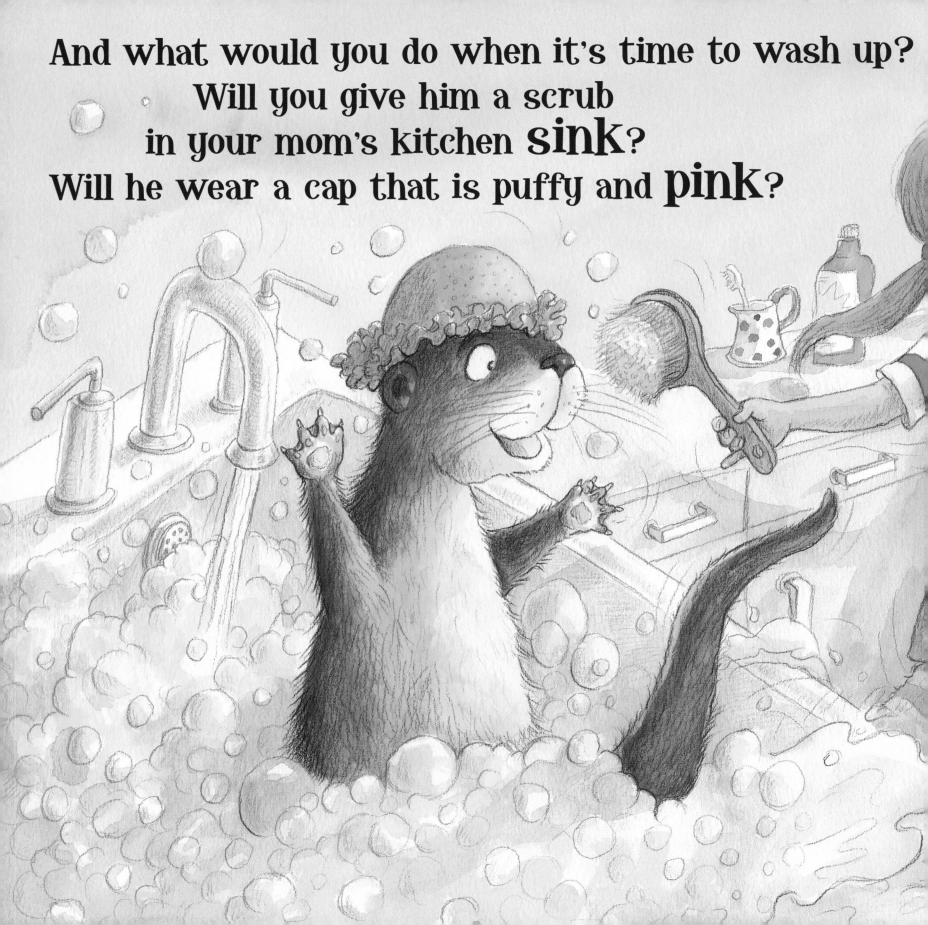

Will he want more **bubbles**?
Will he bring you **troubles**?
What will you do when it's
time to wash up?

"This silly **otter** belongs in the **water**.
He cannot **roam**.
His family is waiting for him to come **home**!"

So what happened to us
on that very next **day**?
We better not **say**.

More otters arrived
and we think
they might **stay**!

minedition

North American edition published 2019 by Michael Neugebauer Publishing Ltd. Hong Kong

Text copyright © 2018 Bruno Hächler
Illustration copyright © 2018 Anastasia Arkhipova

Michael Neugebauer Publishing Ltd.,
Unit 28, 5/F, Metro Centre, Phase 2, No.21 Lam Hing Street, Kowloon Bay, Kowloon, Hong Kong
Phone: +852 2807 1711, e-mail: info@minedition.com
This book was printed in May 2019 at L.Rex Ltd
3/F., Blue Box Factory Building, 25 Hing Wo Street, Tin Wan, Aberdeen, Hong Kong, China
Typesetting in Tiffany
Library of Congress Cataloging-in-Publication Data available upon request.

ISBN 978-988-8341-63-4
10 9 8 7 6 5 4 3 2 1
First impression

For more information please visit our website: www.minedition.com

Bruno Hächler

The Teddy Bears' Christmas Surprise

Anastasia Arkhipova

minedition

It was Christmas Eve. A teddy bear with a red bow tie sat forgotten on the bookshelf, waiting for something to happen. He had been waiting there for years. His fur had become dull and shaggy, but his eyes still glinted like they did when he was first held in a child's arms.

He was the first bear to disappear.

Quietly he made his way outside. He shivered in the cold winter wind. But he hunched up his shoulders and set off, determined. When he reached the abandoned shed, he waited.

All over town other bears had slipped away, too. They tiptoed out of children's rooms, squeezed out of toy chests, and climbed down from shop window displays.

One after another they came-fleecy bears with
friendly faces, elegant bears with fancy clothes,
bears with frizzy or velvet fur, and
tiny angel bears-an endless stream.

Just as they were assembled, the bells
in the church tower struck midnight.

Satisfied, the first bear looked around. Not a single bear was missing.

He nodded silently. That was the sign. Within moments, thousands of bears burst outside and spread throughout the town, eager to begin their work.

They climbed over fences and balconies, slid down chimneys, and crawled through doggie doors. They headed straight for the gifts that were wrapped and ready for Christmas morning.

Swiftly the bears unwrapped all the presents and removed what they found–bottles of perfume, building blocks, ice skates, model airplanes, and paint sets. They piled everything into their own bags. Then they slipped little notes they had written in their squiggly bear writing into each box before wrapping them all up again.

When the bears had finished, they returned to their places in children's rooms, toy chests, and shop windows.

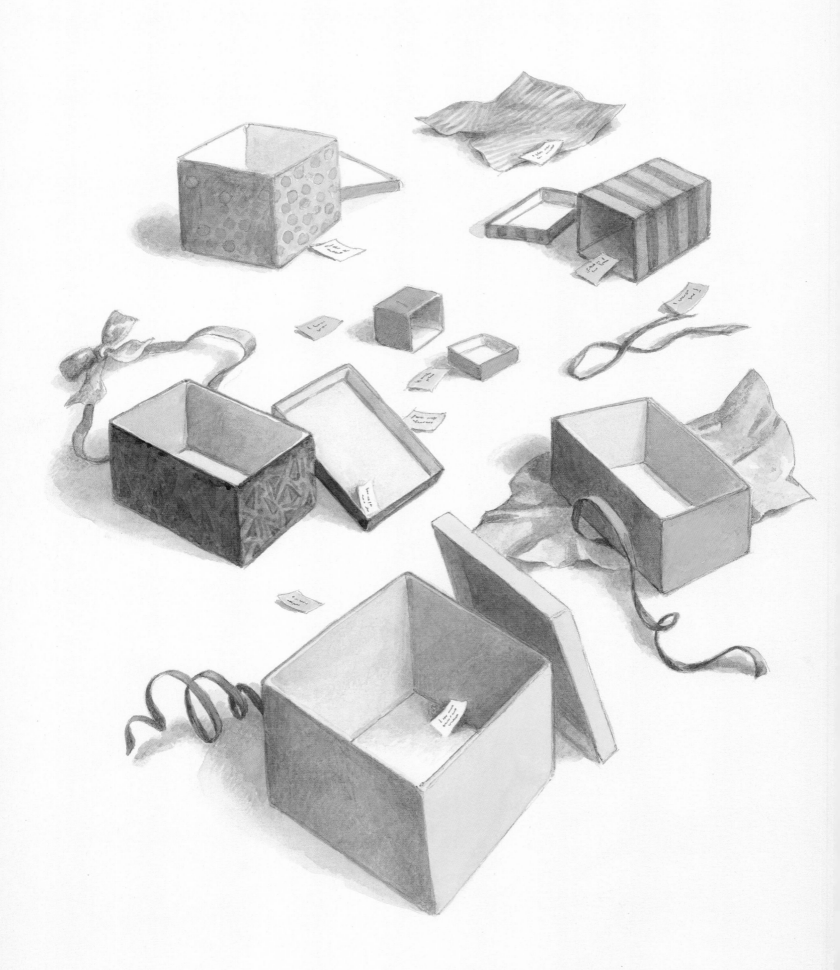

The bears' Christmas surprise caused quite an uproar. Children wept with disappointment when they found only slips of paper instead of toys in their boxes. Parents ran to their neighbors for help, but in each house it was the same story. The gifts were all gone, and no one knew where. No one could explain what had happened.

The people sat for a long time, bewildered. Then they read what was written on the mysterious notes. At first they didn't understand. But as they read the messages again and again, their hearts began to feel lighter, and their disappointment melted away.

The bears had written things like:

> *I love you.*
>
> I often think of you.
>
> *I'll visit you soon.*

And suddenly the people thought about the many lonley people who lived in their town. How awful to be alone and forgotten on Christmas Day!

Without another moment's hesitation, they put on their warmest coats and set out.

They visited grandmothers in the nursing homes, aunts who sat alone in front of the TV, a man who missed his own family terribly. Not a single person in town was overlooked.

Soon laughter and music rang from brightly lit windows everywhere. Together they sang songs and told stories. And over and over the same phrase could be heard:

"MERRY CHRISTMAS!"

That night the people of the town slept deeply and peaceful. They smiled because they'd experienced a real Christmas wonder. And while they were sleeping, the teddy bears returned the presents they had taken back under the Christmas trees.

The bear with the red bow tie is still sitting on the bookshelf. His fur looks even shaggier than before. But his eyes are glinting like on the very first day...